stery Mob
and the Great
Pancake Day Race

Roger Hurn

Illustrated by
Stik

Rising Stars UK Ltd.
22 Grafton Street, London W1S 4EX
www.risingstars-uk.com

The right of Roger Hurn to be identified as the author of this work
has been asserted by him in accordance with the Copyright,
Design and Patents Act 1988.

Published 2008

Text, design and layout © Rising Stars UK Ltd.

Cover design: Burville-Riley Partnership
Illustrator: Stik, Bill Greenhead for Illustration Ltd
Text design and typesetting: Andy Wilson
Publisher: Gill Budgell
Editor: Catherine Baker

British Library Cataloguing in Publication Data.
A CIP record for this book is available from the British Library

ISBN: 978-1-84680-426-7

Printed in the UK by CPI Bookmarque, Croydon, CR0 4TD

Mixed Sources
Product group from well-managed
forests and other controlled sources
www.fsc.org Cert no. TT-COC-002227
© 1996 Forest Stewardship Council

Contents

Meet the Mystery Mob

Name:

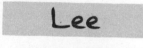
Gummy

FYI: Gummy hasn't got much brain – and even fewer teeth.

Loves: Soup.

Hates: Toffee chews.

Fact: The brightest thing about him is his shirt.

Name:

Lee

FYI: If Lee was any cooler he'd be a cucumber.

Loves: Hip-hop.

Hates: Hopscotch.

Fact: He has his own designer label (which he peeled off a tin).

Name:

Rob

FYI: Rob lives in his own world – he's just visiting planet Earth.

Loves: Daydreaming.

Hates: Nightmares.

Fact: Rob always does his homework – he just forgets to write it down.

Name:

Dwayne

FYI: Dwayne is smarter than a tree full of owls.

Loves: Anything complicated.

Hates: Join-the-dots books.

Fact: If he was any brighter you could use him as a floodlight at football matches.

Name:

Chet

FYI: Chet is as brave as a lion with steel jaws.

Loves: Having adventures.

Hates: Knitting.

Fact: He's as tough as the chicken his granny cooks for his tea.

Name:

Adi

FYI: Adi is as happy as a football fan with tickets to the big match.

Loves: Telling jokes.

Hates: Moaning minnies.

Fact: He knows more jokes than a jumbo joke book.

Flipping Pancakes

The Perfect Pancake Café is holding
a Great Pancake Race on Pancake Day.
The first prize is free pancakes for a year!

Gummy I sooo want to win the Great
Pancake Race. Imagine it.
Free pancakes for a year!
Now that's what I call a prize.
Man, I can almost taste
those pancakes now ...

Dwayne Everybody wants to win
the Great Pancake Race, Gum,
but it won't be easy. You have to
go on a cross-country run
while tossing a pancake in a pan.

Gummy Yeah, I know that. But I'm
a good runner.

Dwayne Really? Lee is a much better
runner than you! It's all
the football training he does.

Gummy Yes, but Lee's not entering the race. He says too many pancakes are bad for footballers.

Dwayne Okay, but Rob's faster than you.

Gummy Huh, he can't run and toss pancakes at the same time. He keeps tripping over his feet.

Dwayne Hmmm … that's true. Hey, but Adi is pretty quick. He'll beat you.

Gummy No, he won't. He burnt his mum's frying pan when he was making pancakes, so she's grounded him.

Dwayne What about Chet? He's good.

Gummy No, he isn't. He likes his pancakes so thick they're too heavy to toss.

Dwayne Well then, Gum, you just might have a chance after all.

Gummy   I hope so, but I'm up against Barry and Harry, the Timms twins. Those two like pancakes almost as much as I do.

Dwayne   No problem. I'll be your trainer, then you'll win for sure.

Gummy   Thanks Dwayne. You're a real mate!

Dwayne   Yes, but if you win I want to share the prize.

Gummy   What!!? That means you get
             to eat half of my pancakes!

Dwayne   (sternly) Too many pancakes
             are not good for you, Gummy.
             So I'm doing you a favour.
             I don't want to eat them –
             but it's my duty as your trainer.

Gummy   Oh. I see. Sorry, Dwayne.

Dwayne   That's okay, Gum.
             Keeping you fit is my job.

Out of the Frying Pan onto the Floor

Dwayne looks in his mum's cookbook
and finds a recipe for Old Mother
Bellybuster's pancake mix. He shows it
to Gummy.

Dwayne   It says in the book that
the winner of the Great Pancake
Race always uses Old Mother
Bellybuster's recipe.

Gummy   Wicked! I'll batter Barry
and Harry with her pancake mix.

Dwayne   No, Gum. You've got to make
a pancake with it – not throw it
at people.

Gummy   Oh, stop worrying. I make
great pancakes.

Dwayne   Yes, but the problem is you keep
eating them.

Gummy   So? That's what you're meant
to do with pancakes.

Dwayne Actually, Gummy, you're meant to eat them *after* you've won the race, not before. If you keep on stuffing them in your mouth as soon as they're cooked, how can you practise running and tossing them?

Gummy Ah, I hadn't thought of that.

Dwayne That's why you need me as your trainer. Now come on, let's see some action!

Gummy makes one of Old Mother
Bellybuster's special pancakes.
It looks so good that Gummy
grabs it and opens his mouth wide.

Dwayne   (shouting) Put that pancake
back in the pan at once!

Gummy   Whoops. Sorry.

Dwayne   All right. But I won't tell you
again.

Gummy   You won't have to. My mouth's
back under control.

Dwayne   Good. Now toss that pancake
and run at the same time.

Gummy flips the pancake up into the air.
It lands on his head.

Dwayne   Doh! Take that pancake off your
head, Gummy.

Gummy   Why? Does it make me look silly?

Dwayne No. Nothing can make you look sillier than you already do.

Gummy (happily) Thanks, Dwayne.

Dwayne That's okay. Now what I want is for you to keep on practising with that pancake. Otherwise you'll never beat Harry and Barry.

Gummy finally gets the hang of running
and tossing the pancake so it lands
back in the pan and not on his head.

Dwayne   (excitedly) He's got it!
By George, I think he's got it!

Gummy   Who's George?

Dwayne   You know – St George.
The one who killed the dragon.

Gummy   Forget dragons. Is he any good at tossing pancakes? And is he in the race?

Dwayne   Er … no.

Gummy   Phew! That's a relief. It's going to be hard enough to beat Harry and Barry. I don't need to be up against George as well.

Pancakes to Go

It's the day of the Great Pancake Race.
Gummy is in his running kit with his
frying pan in his hand. He has
the number 123 on his shirt. He stands
next to Harry on the start line.
Harry is number 124.

Gummy   Hi, Harry. Where's Barry?

Harry   He's at home in bed. He's sick.

Gummy Hmm ... I bet he ate too many pancakes in training.

Harry Whatever. But I'll still beat you. That prize is going to be mine.

Gummy I don't think so, Harry. In fact, I've only got one thing to say to you.

Harry What's that?

Gummy Bake my day!

The race starts and Gummy and Harry
zoom off. Dwayne follows them on his
bike. Harry goes into the lead.
Gummy overtakes him.

Dwayne   Keep going, Gum.
            Harry is miles behind.

Gummy   This race is in the bag.

The road makes a tight turn at Twister's
Bend. Gummy and Dwayne get a big
surprise when they come out of it.
Harry's in front of them!

Dwayne Hey, there's Harry.
He's back in the lead!

Gummy How did he do that?

Dwayne I've no idea. Maybe he took
a short cut.

Gummy Okay, don't worry. I'll soon
catch up with him.

Gummy overtakes Harry again.

Gummy See you back at the finish,
Harry.

Dwayne Don't panic, Harry.
Gummy'll save a pancake
for you.

Harry Grrr!

Now the road goes through Witches
Wood. Gummy and Dwayne
hurtle through it. But, when they come
out of the wood, Harry is in front
of them again.

Gummy   He's done it again!
              But I'll still beat him.

Dwayne   Go for it, Gum.

Gummy puts on a sprint and runs
past Harry.

Gummy Give up, Harry. You're getting
on my nerves.

Dwayne You've got no chance of Gummy
saving you a pancake now.

Harry Grrrr!

It's Impossible

Dwayne There's something wrong here, Gum.

Gummy What? I haven't dropped my pancake once!

Dwayne So how does Harry keep on overtaking you without us seeing him do it?

Gummy I don't know. You're the trainer. You figure it out.

Dwayne That's just what I'm going to do.

Dwayne rides off on his bike up towards
the finish line. He cycles past the bus
shelter. He sees Harry hiding behind it!
Dwayne can hardly believe his eyes.
He pedals as fast as he can back
to Gummy.

Dwayne Don't drop your pancake when
I tell you this, but I've just seen
Harry up ahead hiding behind
the bus shelter.

Gummy You can't have done. Harry's way behind me in the race. I'm beating him easily.

Dwayne And I'm telling you he's way ahead of you up at the bus shelter.

Gummy But that's impossible. Harry can't be in two places at once.

Dwayne You're right. He can't.

Gummy   So what's happening then?
Is he in front of me or not?

Dwayne   That's what I'm off to find out.
I've got an idea what Harry's
up to, but I'll need the other lads
to help me prove it. This is
definitely a job for the
Mystery Mob.

Dwayne cycles off. Gummy keeps
on running and tossing his pancake.
As he gets near to the bus shelter,
he sees Harry jump out from behind it
and race away at top speed.

Gummy (shouting) Oi! I don't know how
you keep getting into the lead,
Harry, but I'll catch you.
You haven't won yet. This race
isn't over till it's over!

The Perfect Ending

The Perfect Pancake Café comes
into view. Gummy is hot on Harry's heels,
but Harry just holds him off to cross
the finish line first.

Harry   Yay! The year's supply
of free pancakes is mine!
Tough luck, loser.

Gummy   Huh! It doesn't bother me.
I prefer waffles anyway.

The crowd clap and Sheila Eatem,
the owner of the Perfect Pancake Café,
steps forward to give Harry his prize.

Sheila   Well done, Harry. Here's your
free ticket for a year's supply
of pancakes.

But before Harry can take it,
Dwayne appears with a boy who looks
exactly like Harry. The boy is scowling.

Dwayne   Hold it, Miss Eatem. That's not
Harry – this is! And if two Harrys
aren't enough for you,
here are two more.

From their hiding place behind the Café,
the Mystery Mob drag out two more boys
who look exactly like Harry. They are
wearing identical running kits to Harry
and have the same number on their vests.

Gummy (gasping) But they all look alike!

Dwayne Of course they do. They're two sets of twins.

Gummy You're kidding me?

Dwayne No, I'm not. These two are Harry and Barry, and these are their cousins Larry and Gary.

Gummy But Harry said Barry was in bed sick.

Dwayne He was fibbing! Harry and Barry didn't fancy their chances of winning, so they made up their minds to win by cheating. And they got Larry and Gary involved in the plot.

Harry All right, I admit it. We figured we'd win the race and then each of us would take it in turns to go to the café to eat pancakes. No one would ever know.

Sheila   Well, we know now. So you haven't won – Gummy has!

The crowd cheer. Gummy and Dwayne and the rest of the Mystery Mob go into the café to tuck into a pile of pancakes, while Harry, Barry, Gary and Larry stand outside feeling flatter than a pancake.

Dwayne Hey, Harry, Barry, Larry
and Gary thought they had
the perfect plan, but we're
the ones who got the perfect
pancakes!

Gummy doesn't reply. He knows
it's rude to talk with your mouth full –
and Gummy's mouth is full
of perfect pancakes!

About the author

Roger Hurn has:

- had a hit record in Turkey
- won *The Weakest Link* on TV
- swum with sharks on the Great Barrier Reef.

Now he's a writer, and he hopes you like reading about the Mystery Mob as much as he likes writing about them.

The great food quiz

Questions

1 How do you make milk shake?

2 Why did the school kid eat his homework?

3 How do you train a dog not to beg for food at the table?

4 What do cats call mice on skateboards?

5 What starts with 't', ends with 't' and is filled with 't'?

6 What kind of biscuits do you get if you put three ducks in a box?

7 Why don't teddy bears eat dessert?

8 Why are chefs cruel?

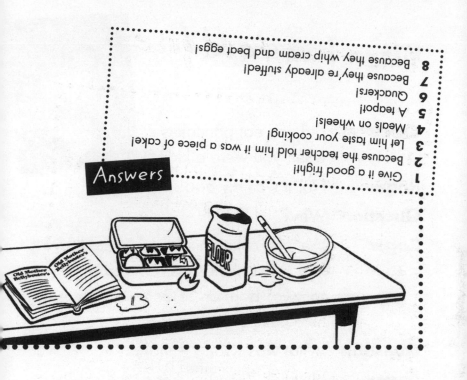

How did you score?

🖐 If you got all eight great food quiz answers correct, then you are a celebrity chef!

🖐 If you got six great food quiz answers correct, then you are really cooking.

🖐 If you got fewer than four great food quiz answers correct, then you're the kind of chef who needs a recipe to boil water!

When I was a kid

Question   Did you eat pancakes
            when you were a kid?

Roger   No. It was my dad's fault.

Question   Why?

Roger   Well, he asked his friends what they
        had called their sons. One said his
        son was born on St George's Day so
        he'd called him George.

Question   What was wrong with that?

Roger   Nothing. Then another friend said
        his son was born on St Patrick's Day
        so he called him Patrick.

Question   So?

Roger   Well, my dad thought that was a
        really clever way to think of a name
        for a son, so he used it when my
        little brother was born.

Question   What was the problem with that?

Roger   Well, my little brother was born on
        Pancake Day.

Adi's favourite pancake race joke

What does the winner of a long-distance pancake race always lose?

Her breath!

How to make Old Mother Bellybuster's perfect pancake

Top Tip – Do not cook these pancakes without an adult's help!

You'll need:
225g plain flour
4 eggs
pinch of salt
400ml milk mixed with 200ml water
1 tablespoon vegetable oil
A knob of butter
Sugar
Lemon juice

What to do:

1 Whisk the milk, eggs and salt together in a bowl.

2 Fold in the sieved flour a little at a time, and whisk until smooth.

3 Slowly melt the butter and then stir into the mix.

4 Heat a small amount of oil in a frying pan until it almost starts to smoke.

5 Pour in enough batter to coat the bottom of the pan thinly.

6 Cook until it reaches a light golden brown colour, then toss the pancake, catch it and cook the other side for a few seconds.

7 If you drop it, try again!

8 Sprinkle your pancake with sugar and lemon juice, and roll it up.

9 Eat it!

Five fantastic facts about Pancake Day

1 A famous pancake race has been held in Olney since 1445. Legend says it started when a woman heard the church bells ringing as she was making pancakes. She didn't want to be late so she raced off to church, carrying her frying pan and pancake!

2 The proper name for Pancake Day is Shrove Tuesday.

3 In parts of Canada, people bake all sorts of things into pancakes on Shrove Tuesday. They say if you find a coin in yours it means you will become rich. But if you find a hair in your pancake – send it back to the chef!

4 The world's biggest pancake was 15.01 metres in diameter, 2.5 cm deep, and weighed 3 metric tonnes. Not even Gummy could eat a pancake that size!

5 Pancake Day is called Mardi Gras in New Orleans. Mardi Gras is French and means 'Fat Tuesday'!

Pancake lingo

Batter The mixture of flour and milk you need to make pancakes – not the person who faces the bowler in cricket.

Cramwyth If you're in Wales and want a pancake, this is the word to use. Just make sure your cramwyth is 'crammed with' good stuff!

Crepe This is a French pancake and should not be confused with a type of thin crinkly paper which is also called crepe. You can soon tell which is which if you try eating them.

Shrove Tuesday Shrove comes from the word 'shrive' meaning to confess. If you burn your mum's frying pan on Shrove Tuesday you'd better confess or she'll be cross.

Mystery Mob

Mystery Mob Set 1:

Mystery Mob and the Abominable Snowman
Mystery Mob and the Big Match
Mystery Mob and the Circus of Doom
Mystery Mob and the Creepy Castle
Mystery Mob and the Haunted Attic
Mystery Mob and the Hidden Treasure
Mystery Mob and the Magic Bottle
Mystery Mob and the Missing Millions
Mystery Mob and the Monster on the Moor
Mystery Mob and the Mummy's Curse
Mystery Mob and the Time Machine
Mystery Mob and the UFO

Mystery Mob Set 2:

Mystery Mob and the Ghost Town
Mystery Mob and the Bonfire Night Plot
Mystery Mob and the April Fools' Day Joker
Mystery Mob and the Great Pancake Day Race
Mystery Mob and the Scary Santa
Mystery Mob and the Conker Conspiracy
Mystery Mob and the Top Talent Contest
Mystery Mob and the Night in the Waxworks
Mystery Mob and the Runaway Train
Mystery Mob and the Wrong Robot
Mystery Mob and the Day of the Dinosaurs
Mystery Mob and the Man-eating Tiger

RISING ★ STARS

Mystery Mob books are available from most booksellers.

**For mail order information
please call Rising Stars on 0871 47 23 010
or visit www.risingstars-uk.com**